HOME FOR
IMAGINARY
FRIENDS™

HOUSE OF BLOO'S

by Pam Pollack and Meg Belviso
Based on "Foster's Home for Imaginary Friends"
as created by Craig McCracken

SCHOLASTIC INC.
New York   Toronto   London   Auckland   Sydney
Mexico City   New Delhi   Hong Kong   Buenos Aires

No part of this publication may be reproduced, or stored in a retrieval system, or transmitted in any form or by any means, electronic, mechanical, photocopying, recording, or otherwise, without written permission of the publisher. For information regarding permission, write to Scholastic Inc., Attention: Permissions Department, 557 Broadway, New York, NY 10012.

ISBN 0-439-75057-1

12 11 10 9 8 7 6 5 4 3 2 1   6 7 8 9 10/0

Printed in the U.S.A.
First printing, January 2006

IT'S MR. DESTRUCTO AND BREAKY

The kitchen was silent. Slowly, the head of a mop-topped boy came up from the back of the counter. The boy was named Mac, and he was scared. Mac's eyes shifted around nervously, trying to make sure that the coast was clear. Then another head came up right next to him. But this was not the head of a boy. This was the round, blue head of Bloo, Mac's Imaginary Friend. Mac and Bloo both shifted their eyes to the left. Then to the right. They thought they were safe. But they were wrong.

Behind them a terrible shadow rose up. A shadow with spiky hair and big ears — and was that an evil smile? The hair on the back of Mac's

neck started to prickle. Bloo had no hair, but his neck rippled with fear. Slowly Mac and Bloo raised their eyes to see . . .

"Terrence!" Mac yelled. It was Mac's horrible bully of an older brother. "Run!"

"Wait!" Terrence shouted. "Stop! I just wanna punch you!"

Furious, Terrence gave chase, forcing his little brother and his friend to race away as fast as they could.

As they went around and around the couch, Bloo called out to his buddy, "Hey, Mac!"

"Yeah?"

"Your brother . . . "

"Yeah?"

"Is a . . ."

"Uh-huh?"

"Big . . . DOOFUS!"

Mac kept running, but now he was laughing, too.

But Terrence didn't think it was funny. He shouted, "Shut up, you . . . you . . ." Terrence

frowned, trying to think. Thinking was not something he did a lot of, because he wasn't very bright. Finally, he came up with what he thought was a brilliant insult: "BLOOFUS!"

Bloo skidded to a stop. That was the dumbest thing he'd ever heard and he just had to say so. "Bloofus?" he said. "Bloofus?!"

"His name is Blooregard Q. Kazoo and you know it, Terrence!" said Mac, scowling up at his much bigger brother.

"Right," said Bloo, joining Mac in taking a stand. "*Bloofus?* How stupid can you get?"

"Shut up!" yelled Terrence, diving over the couch. A second later, he rose up with Mac under one arm and Bloo under the other. Mac kicked his feet, trying to get free. Bloo wiggled his jelly body.

"Well, well, well." Terrence laughed. "What have we got here? It's Mr. Destructo!" He lifted Mac higher. "And his evil pal, Breaky! Mom is gonna be so mad when she sees what you two have done!"

"But we haven't done anything!" Bloo insisted.

"Oh, no?" asked Terrence. Grabbing Bloo by the top of his round head, Terrence smashed him into a table lamp. It shattered into a million pieces. Bloo had sure done something now. "Breaky!" Terrence wailed. "How could you?"

Bloo gritted his teeth and struggled against Terrence's grip. He couldn't get free!

"Stop it, Terrence!" Mac shouted.

"But I'm not doing anything," Terrence said nastily. "It's MR. DESTRUCTO AND BREAKY! Mwa-ha-ha-ha!"

Using Mac and Bloo as his weapons, Mr. Destructo and Breaky, Terrence destroyed every inch of the room. He punched Mr. Destructo's feet into the VCR, shoved Breaky into a lamp, pulled down the hanging plant,

sent CDs flying, and shattered the framed picture of Mac and Bloo.

The real Mac and Bloo kicked and struggled but couldn't break out of Terrence's grasp.

Having more fun than ever, Terrence stretched out his arms and spun Mac and Bloo around faster and faster. Mac thought he was going to be sick. But then Bloo spotted something high up on a cabinet: Mom's favorite vase. Bloo knew she would hate it if anything happened to it. Bloo's eyes brightened as he got an idea. "Woo-hoo!" he yelled happily. "This rules! Break more! Break more!"

"Bloo, no!" yelled Mac.

"Quiet, you!" said Bloo with a fiendish gleam in his eye. Mac watched in horror. It looked like

Bloo had actually turned to the dark side — Terrence's side.

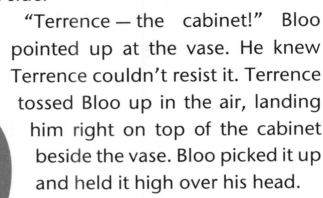

"Terrence — the cabinet!" Bloo pointed up at the vase. He knew Terrence couldn't resist it. Terrence tossed Bloo up in the air, landing him right on top of the cabinet beside the vase. Bloo picked it up and held it high over his head.

"Break it! Break it!" said Terrence.

Bloo smiled wickedly. "Sorry, Mac," he said. "I hate to *break it* to ya, but . . . " Bloo hurled the vase. Mac watched horrified, as it spun down. But then it landed right on Terrence's head. Bull's-eye! Terrence was out cold on the floor.

Bloo jumped lightly down from the cabinet and landed beside his friend. "Your brother is a big fat doofus."

"Hurray!" Mac yelled, happy that his lousy brother had finally gotten what he deserved.

He and Bloo danced around. "Oh, yeah! Oh, yeah! We won! Big doofus! Oh, yeah!"

They were so happy, they didn't hear the key in the front door.

Mom was home.

BLOO GETS THE BLUES

2

With destruction all around them and Terrence knocked out on the floor, Mac and Bloo were totally caught — there was no getting out of this one.

"Mom, it's not what you . . ." said Mac.

"Yeah," said Bloo. "It was Terrence. He . . ."

"Mommy!" Terrence sat up suddenly with a piece of broken vase on his head. "Mac and Bloo were meeeeean to me!" Terrence grabbed Mom around her knees and hugged her close. "I was bein' a good boy when Bloo started to tear the house apart! I tried to stop him, but when Mac joined in, they started beating on me!"

Mac's and Bloo's mouths dropped open in amazement.

Bloo waved his blobby arm in desperation. "That is SO not what happened! Terrence —"

"Is the oldest," Mom cut in. "And is in charge of the house when I'm not home."

"Ha!" said Terrence viciously from around Mom's leg.

"And," Mom continued, "I expect him to act like the oldest and *tell the truth.*"

"Ha!" cried Mac and Bloo, knowing that Terrence could never tell the truth.

"But, Mom," Terrence whined, "I was telling the —"

"Terrence," Mom said. "You expect me to believe that a thirteen-year-old boy was overpowered by an eight-year-old and his cute little Imaginary Friend?"

"Yeah," Bloo said, gesturing. "Mac's a wimp."

"And Bloo's spineless," Mac agreed.

Bloo wiggled all over to illustrate.

"I've had a long day," Mom sighed. "Terrence,

go to your room."

Furious, Terrence clomped off to his room. Mac and Bloo made faces of victory as he went.

"Mac! Bloo! That's enough!" Mom said sharply. "I'm fed up with the three of you always fighting. Mac, I need to talk to you. Alone."

"It's okay, Mac," Bloo reassured him. "I'll be right here. I'm not going anywhere."

Mac followed Mom down the hall to his room. She shut the door behind them. Bloo listened at the door.

"Mac," said Mom. "You know how tired I am of you three fighting."

"Mom! Terrence always picks on me and treats me like a baby!"

"And why do you think he does that?"

Mac didn't seem to know what she meant, so Mom added, "Maybe because of Bloo?"

"Bloo? Why?" asked Mac.

"Because, Mac, you're eight years old and you still have your Imaginary Friend!"

"So what?" said Mac. "Lots of kids have Imaginary Friends. You even had one when you were little!"

"Yes, when I was *little*," Mom said patiently. "But by the time I was your age, I didn't need my Imaginary Friend anymore."

"What are you saying?" asked Mac.

"I think it's time you got rid of Bloo," Mom said. "You need to grow up and say good-bye to Bloo."

"But, Mom, we're best friends," he said. "I promise I'll be good! I'll keep Bloo locked in my room."

"Mac," Mom said. "You're too old for him. You have got to get rid of Bloo."

Now Bloo's mouth dropped open in complete shock. Suddenly a spitwad hit him in the eye.

Bloo looked across the hall. There was Terrence, sitting smugly on his bed, straw in hand, ready to blow more spitwads. Terrence waved to Bloo. *"Hasta la bye-bye,"* he said, laughing his dumb, evil laugh.

That night a miserable Bloo sat in the top bunk over Mac's. He slowly flipped the channels on the TV, looking for something to take his mind off this terrible situation, until he landed on a commercial for a place called Foster's.

"Foster's Home for Imaginary Friends is a wonderful, fun-derful imagination habitation," the ad promised. "We provide food, shelter, and a warm heart for Imaginary Friends looking for a place to call home. So if you have, or know of, an Imaginary Friend in desperate need of a home, come on down to Foster's, where good ideas are not forgotten!"

Bloo looked at the house pictured on the television. It was an awesome Victorian-style house with a high tower and a flag blowing in

the breeze. It had an iron fence in front of it and a big tree in the yard.

If they welcomed Imaginary Friends at this house, it was definitely his kind of place.

FOSTER'S HOME FOR IMAGINARY FRIENDS

3

The next day, Bloo took Mac over to this place called Foster's. "The commercial said it was some fantasma-astical magical place!" Bloo said excitedly as he walked through the big iron gate. But Mac didn't look quite as happy as Bloo.

Bloo knocked on the big wooden door, continuing to try and sell Mac on the idea. "With me living here, Mom will be happy, Terrence will leave you alone, and you can visit me every day. It's perfect. Our problems are solved!"

The door was opened by an enormous bunny. He wore a checked waistcoat, a red bow tie, and a little top hat. He had a monocle in

one eye. "Good day, gentlemen," said the rabbit. He had a very proper English accent. "How may I be of assistance?"

Mac and Bloo looked up in amazement.

"Cool!" said Bloo. "A bunny butler!"

"My good man!" said the bunny. "I am Mr. Herriman, the head of business affairs at this facility. I am in no way a butler or any other member of the service trade! Now if you would please state your business."

"Well, Mr. Rabbitman," said Bloo, pushing himself through the door.

"Herriman!"

"Well, Mr. Herriman," continued Bloo, launching into a big sob story, "my boy, Mac, has the worst life ever! This poor kid lives all alone with me, his mother, and his jerky brother in this trashy, rundown dump of an apartment!"

Knowing this wasn't true, Mac tried to protest, but Bloo just kept on going with his crazy story.

"His brother, who's eight feet tall and weighs three hundred pounds," Bloo went on, totally overexaggerating, "beats up little, wimpy Mac all the time!" Bloo punched poor Mac in the stomach to illustrate. "There's no one to stop him, 'cause his mom works fifteen jobs a week, including weekends. So, yeah, each and every day, Mac is killed dead by his big stupid brother."

"Huh?" said a confused Mac.

But Bloo continued his tall tale. "All this kid has is me, his best buddy, Bloo. But get this. His mother says he's too old for an Imaginary Friend. So I'm at your mercy, kind sir. Can you find it in your big bunny heart to open up your home to this rejected Imaginary Friend?"

Bloo looked up at Herriman wide-eyed and desperate. Mr. Herriman, however, was not moved.

"I shall arrange a tour," said Herriman. He hopped over to a

big horn on the wall and spoke into it. "Miss Frances! Your presence is requested in the foyer. There are two gentlemen here in need of a tour. Miss Fran —"

"I'M COMING!" someone screeched through the other end of the horn. "Sheesh!"

"She'll be with you momentarily," said Herriman. He hopped back to his office.

After a few minutes, a hip-looking young woman came down the stairs. Her red hair was pulled into a ponytail and she wore a green hoodie sweatshirt, a short skirt, and sneakers. "Whatever the bunny said was wrong. My name's not Frances, it's Frankie. I'll give you the tour. Foster's was founded in —"

Suddenly a rude, demanding voice hollered over the horn, "Frankie! Get up here, now!"

Frankie sighed. "Sorry, guys," she said. "Her

Royal Highness calls — that's Duchess. I'll get someone to show you around." Frankie turned, yelling to someone Mac and Bloo couldn't see. "Hey, Wilt! Tour, please!" She turned back to Mac and Bloo. "Wilt will take care of you, and I'll meet up with you at the end." A frustrated Frankie headed upstairs.

"Hey, how you doing?" someone unseen said. "Name's Wilt."

Mac and Bloo looked up . . . and up and up at this supertall Imaginary Friend who called himself Wilt. He was bright red, with a number 1 on his chest. He had googly eyes, one of which was not working like it should. His arms and legs were very long, except for his left arm, which was cut off and sewn up.

Mac and Bloo stared up at him, stunned.

Wilt looked down at them.

Nobody said anything.

Finally Wilt broke the ice. "Okay, I get it. It's cool. I know I'm all broken with the wonky eye and the stubby arm. Probably freaks you out, huh? Don't sweat it. I'll get somebody else to give you a tour."

But Mac and Bloo weren't staring at Wilt because of his wonky eye or his stubby arm. They were amazed for one reason.

"You're tall," Mac and Bloo said together. "You should play basketball."

"Thanks," said Wilt. "How 'bout that tour?"

And so the amazing Wilt took them on the most amazing tour of the most amazing house ever. He took them through the waiting room, living room, sitting room, and parlor. Each place was weirder and cooler than the last. But then Wilt had to stop. He had to show them a picture of Madame Foster, a tiny old lady with white hair and glasses. She'd started Foster's Home for Imaginary Friends. If it wasn't for her,

who knows what would've happened to all these Imaginary Friends.

In the kitchen, they ran into an Imaginary Friend that looked like a combination bird, airplane, and palm tree. "Coco?" it said.

"No, thanks," said Mac.

"Coco?" it said to Bloo.

"Yes," said Bloo, who never turned down a cup of cocoa.

To his confusion, the creature asked, "Coco?" again.

"Yes," Bloo repeated.

"Coco?"

"Yes."

Now Bloo was annoyed. Hadn't he already told her he wanted cocoa? "Yes," he said impatiently. "With marshmallows, please!"

"Sorry," said Wilt, who had to explain this a lot. "That's Coco. She's not asking you if you want cocoa. *All she says is* Coco."

"Oh!" said Bloo. "So what was she saying really?"

"She wanted to know if you wanted any juice."

Pleased by this new and unusual friend, Mac and Bloo continued their tour with Wilt and Coco. But when Mac stopped to tie his shoe on the fourth floor, he had the strange feeling that somebody was watching him. Mac could have sworn he saw a big sharp horn pointing around the corner. But when Mac looked closer, it was gone.

Wilt continued his tour, taking Mac and Bloo

to the music room, playroom, rumpus room, and arcade. Then he opened door after door after door of bedrooms. Behind one bedroom door was Frankie, who was being yelled at by the strangest, creepiest-looking Imaginary Friend Mac and Bloo had ever seen. Her mouth was sidewise, she had a short elephant's trunk for a nose, and her eyes were crooked. She wore a turban, high heels, and lots of jewels. She looked like a nightmare come to life. And acted like it, too. "Get out!" she screamed when she noticed Mac and the friends staring from the hallway. She closed the door with a slam.

"That was Duchess," Wilt explained. "She thinks she's the greatest idea ever thought of, but if you ask me, she's one of the worst."

Mac would have agreed, only he'd just seen that thing

again. Seeing a little more this time, Mac was sure whatever was following him had to be a monster. "Hey, Wilt," he asked nervously. "Are there any monsters here?"

"Actually," Wilt said, "there are. I'll show you." Wilt took them to the backyard past a corral filled with really fantastical unicorns and flying horse Imaginary Friends, to where there was a big scary-looking container with chains all around. Something was growling and struggling inside, fighting to get out. "This is the Extremasaurus," said Wilt. "It's a vicious, destructive Imaginary Friend created by a jerky teenage boy. Don't get too close," he warned.

But it was too late. Just as Wilt was leading Mac and Bloo away, a giant tentacle made of big metal cannonballs snaked out the barred window, grabbing Mac and swinging him through the air.

"*Aaaaaaaaaah!*" Mac screamed in total terror.

HELLLLP!!!!

Mac!" yelled Bloo, terrified for his best friend.

Wilt hopped from one stilty leg to the other, unsure of what to do in the situation but positive that this was not a good way to end a tour. "I'm sorry! I'm sorry! I'm sorry!"

Coco was also completely frazzled and ran around in a circle shouting, "Coco! Coco! Coco!"

From way up in the air, in the Extremasaurus's grasp, Mac spotted another monster running toward him. This monster was purple and hairy, with giant horns coming out of his head. He had big fangs and was roaring like a

bull. His only clothes were a pair of gray pants held up with a belt that had a buckle that looked just like a human skull! It was the monster Mac had seen following them through the entire tour.

"*Rrrraaauuurrrgh!*" bellowed the monster, ramming his horns into the Extremasaurus's cage. The tentacle let go of Mac. He fell through the air and landed right in the hairy purple monster's arms.

"Let him go!" yelled Bloo, punching at the purple monster. "You big stupid monster!"

"*Aaarrrgh!*" the monster wailed. "I no monster!" He ran off, holding Mac under his arm like a football.

Bloo ran after him, shaking his blob of a fist. "No, Bloo!" Wilt called, trying to stop him. "It's okay!"

The monster yelled, "The little blue man *es loco*!"

Coco talked calmly to the purple monster. "Coco? Coco coco coco coco."

"*Sí. Sí.*" The monster listened to Coco, slowing down to a stop. "*Gracias,* Coco," he said, and he finally put Mac down.

"*Aaaaarrrgh!*" Bloo leaped onto the monster and bit him. The monster tried to shake Bloo off, but Bloo wouldn't let go.

"Bloo, no!" called Mac. "I think he's cool!"

"*¡Sí!*" said the monster. "I cool!" And seeing the kindness in the monster's eyes, it was clear that he was cool. "The little boy, he gets swung around and around and . . . it so scary! I try to . . . how you say? I try to help! Please, little crazy blue man. I am good guy! I am friend!"

"Friend?" said a confused Bloo, still holding on to the monster with his teeth.

Wilt stepped in to explain — Wilt was really good at explaining. "This is Eduardo. He wouldn't hurt a fly."

"Why were you being so sneaky?" asked Mac. "And hiding from us all day?"

"I am, how you say? Scared of little kid. I also afraid you would not like me. And so I hide."

"Not *like* you?" said Mac. "Are you crazy? You're a hero, Eduardo!"

"We're all friends here. And speaking of friends," said Wilt, finishing up his tour. "You should see all the Imaginary Friends we've got here at Foster's. We've got friends with horns," he said, walking them past a stable full of pink and purple unicorns. "Friends with wings, friends with horns and wings, friends with horns and wings that talk . . ." He gave some hay to a winged unicorn.

"We've got simple ones, stealthy ones, two-in-ones. Even unimaginative ones. Some kids can't make things up so they just copy what they see on TV. What are you going to do?" Wilt sighed.

There were so many Imaginary Friends, Mac could hardly keep track. But Wilt knew them

all. "Big, small, young, old, happy, sad, good, and bad."

"And don't forget," said Bloo, joining in as they got to the foyer and pointing to his new friends Coco, Eduardo, and Wilt, "silly, nervous, helpful . . ."

"And now," said Mac, finally giving in to Bloo's idea, "Bloo."

"You mean it?" said Bloo.

"Yeah," said Mac. "You can stay."

"*Woo-hoo!*" Bloo danced around and jumped on Mac. "This is so awesome!"

Coco was so happy, she ran around laying brightly colored eggs with prizes inside. One of them even contained a vase just like the one Bloo had broken at home. "Whenever she gets excited, she lays eggs like that," Wilt explained.

"This place is crazy!" said Bloo. "I love it!"

"I guess you dug the tour?" said Frankie, coming down the stairs.

"It's perfect, just like Bloo said," Mac exclaimed. "With him living here, my mom will be happy, Terrence will leave me alone, and I can visit him every day. Our problems are solved."

But their problems weren't solved. . . .

"Um, there is one little thing," said Frankie nervously. "Foster's is a *foster* home. That means nobody lives here forever. If you leave Bloo here, he'll be put up for adoption like everybody else. He'll become some other kid's Imaginary Friend."

"Yeah," said Wilt. "As much as we love living here, what we really want is to be adopted by a new kid who wants an Imaginary Friend."

"Forget it!" said Bloo, heading for the door. "As cool as this place is, adoption is not an option. Come on, Mac. Let's go."

"Wait," said Mac. "What else can we do? Mom said!"

"But . . ." Bloo stared at him in horror. Was Mac actually going to abandon him?

"Just stay here until I can figure something out," said Mac. "What if I come back tomorrow?" he asked Frankie desperately.

"Well, he's still yours," she said uneasily. "But if a kid wants him and you're not here, he will be adopted."

"Okay," said Mac.

"Okay!" repeated Bloo. He couldn't believe what he was hearing.

"I'll be back," Mac assured Bloo. He gathered up the eggs Coco had given him and headed for the door. "I promise!"

Mr. Herriman shut the door with a bang.

"I'll be back," he sniffed with disbelief. "If I had a carrot for every time I'd heard that, I'd be a very fat rabbit! *Hmmmph!*" But even though the bunny didn't believe Mac, he did have some words of assurance. "Don't worry, Master Bloo. You'll be snatched up by a new child in no time."

Bloo sadly pressed his face up to the window and watched Mac walk away.

When Mac got home, a smug Terrence was waiting for him. "Hey, stupid," he said, smacking Mac in the back of his head. "Where were you, stupid? What are those stupid eggs, stupid? Where's that stupid little blue friend of yours, stupid? If you didn't get rid of him, you're gonna be so busted!"

Mac whirled around angrily. "I was nowhere! They're nothing! And I took care of it! Happy?" He slammed the door to his room, tossed the eggs in his closet, and climbed into bed. He pulled the covers up to his chin and

gazed at the picture of Bloo on his bedside table.

Meanwhile at Foster's, Bloo got ready for bed with Wilt, Coco, and Eduardo. Wilt and Eduardo shared a bunk bed. Coco had a nest in the corner. But there was no bed for Bloo.

"Oh!" said Wilt, realizing that this new friend didn't have a proper place to sleep. "I'm sorry. Take my bunk!" The long-legged Wilt then crawled under the bed, sleeping on the floor without complaint. His feet stuck out at one end.

Coco settled into her nest. Eduardo crawled into the top bunk and leaned his head down to Bloo. "*Buenas noches, Azul,*" he said.

"Don't worry," Wilt called from under the bed. "Mac will come back."

Bloo gave a weak smile, hoping it was true.

But he was still worried and couldn't sleep. Suddenly something came flying at him from out of the dark. It was one of Coco's eggs. Bloo opened it up to find a picture of Mac inside for his bedside table. He smiled at the picture and fell asleep at last.

TIFFANY

5

Early the next morning, Mr. Herriman called Frankie on the horn. There was a family downstairs who wanted to adopt an Imaginary Friend.

All the Imaginary Friends went running to the lobby, hoping today was their day to be adopted. Realizing this was the one thing that couldn't happen, Bloo tried to stay behind, but a stampede of friends swept him into the foyer. Frankie squeezed through the crowd of Imaginary Friends to greet the very rich, very snooty new family. "How can I help you?"

"My daughter's in need of an Imaginary Friend," said the father with his nose in the air.

"Shuddup, Dad!" screamed the bratty little girl, her hands balled into fists. She stamped her foot. "I just don't think I should hafta waste my time when I can just *buy* one."

"Having an Imaginary Friend isn't like buying a toy," said Frankie. She had seen kids like this before. She knew they were trouble. "It's a big responsibility —"

"Yeah, yeah. Whatever," snapped the girl. "Just get me an Imaginary Friend. And not a cheap one, either!"

"So," her dad drawled, "do you have a friend for my precious little sweetums or what?"

"Out of my vay! Out of my vay!" Duchess rudely pushed her way through the crowd.

Frankie couldn't believe her luck. Finally. The perfect family to adopt Duchess — rich and snooty. "Here's just the friend for your precious little sweetums! Presenting Her Royal Duchess, Diamond Persnickitty the First, Last, and Only."

"My papers," said Duchess, handing over some official papers.

"Hmmm," said the father. "A pedigreed Imaginary Friend. Very valuable!"

Frankie desperately dragged the couple into Herriman's office to draw up the paperwork.

Realizing today wasn't their day, the Imaginary Friends filed out of the hallway, leaving Bloo by himself on the stairs. "Hey, guys?" he said. "Guys? Oh."

Bloo and the bratty little girl were alone in the foyer. Bloo trembled in fear as she stalked across the hall and loomed over him. "Nice little girl," he said nervously. "Go away now. Shoo! Shoo!"

The girl leaned down into his face. She took a deep breath and yelled, "SHUT UP! I LIKE YOU! YOU'RE CUTE! I'M GONNA ADOPT YOU! YOU'RE GONNA BE MY FRIEND AND I'M GONNA CALL YOU TIFFANY! YOU GOT THAT, TIFFANYYYYYY?!!!!"

"No!" whimpered Bloo. "HEEEELLLLLPP!!!"

Just as she was about to pounce on Bloo, he was picked up by . . .

"Eduardo!"

Eduardo tucked Bloo under one arm and ran like he was going for a touchdown, until he reached Wilt, who stretched out a long red arm and took him.

"COME BACK HERE WITH MY TIFFANY!!" yelled the brat.

Wilt ran like he was going for a jump shot — until he tripped over Coco's big foot, went flying, and crashed into the wall. So Coco grabbed Bloo and took off. "Coco!"

"WHERE'S MY TIFFANY, YOU FREAK?" the girl demanded. She ran off after Coco and Bloo. Wilt ran after Coco. Eduardo ran after Wilt.

They raced from one room to another, through dozens of doors, this way and that, passing Bloo around over and over again. The little brat finally raised Bloo over her head in triumph.

"Now I've got you, my CUTE LITTLE TIF-FANY!" she screeched.

"Uh, guys?" Bloo called to Wilt, Coco, and Eduardo. "A little help, please?"

"SHUT UP, TIFFANY!" she screeched, stomping off to Mr. Herriman's office.

Mr. Herriman was just finishing up the paperwork for Duchess to be adopted by the snooty family.

"You are making a very vise investment," cooed Duchess. "For I am a verk of art."

Suddenly the door flew open.

"Well, hello, sweetums," her father drawled. "Come meet your new Imaginary Friend."

The girl looked at Duchess with disgust. "EWW! SHE'S UGLY! I HATE HER!"

Frankie snorted, unable to help herself.

"I want this one!" The girl held up Bloo, who was shaking in fear.

Wilt, Coco, and Eduardo dropped to their knees. "Take me instead!" they cried.

"No!" said the girl. "You're broken," she said, walking by Wilt. "You're a chicken," she said as she passed Eduardo. "And you . . ." she said to Coco. "You're a crazy chicken."

"Very well," said Mr. Herriman. "If you'll just sign here, Blooregard will be yours."

"No!" the Imaginary Friends cried, collapsing in an unhappy heap.

39

"That's enough, guys," said Frankie sadly. "If this little girl really wants Tiff — I mean, Bloo . . ."

"I guess it's true. Mac doesn't want me after all," said Bloo, bowing his head sadly. He finally had to admit that he really had been forgotten.

BEST ENEMIES

6

"**N**ot want you? What are you, crazy?" came a voice from outside the office. It was Mac, standing in the doorway with his backpack.

"Mac!" Bloo's eyes lit up at the sight of his best friend. He stuck his tongue out at the bratty little girl and ran up to him. "Do you have any idea what I've been through all day? Where *were* you?"

"School," said Mac casually.

"Oh, yeah," said Bloo. He felt dumb for ever worrying about Mac leaving him.

The other Imaginary Friends marched around the office happily chanting, "Mac's back! Mac's back! Mac's back!"

"Sorry, sweetums," Frankie said, "but Bloo is Mac's idea and since Mac's here, Bloo's no longer up for adoption. But," Frankie added hopefully, "you can still have Duchess."

"No! I hate her!" The little girl stomped out with her parents behind her.

Duchess watched in fury as her hope for escaping the house marched down the front lane.

"That leetle blue creep ruined my vun chance to get out of here!" the Duchess sniffed as she tottered out on her high heels.

Frankie watched from Herriman's window as Mac and the friends played outside. She saw something different in this kid.

"Mac's not gonna abandon his Imaginary Friend," Frankie said.

"Of course he will," said Mr. Herriman stuffily. "Every child tires of their Imaginary Friend eventually."

Frankie grinned slyly and leaned down to

whisper in his floppy ear. "Yours didn't," she reminded him, winking at the portrait of Madame Foster on the wall.

When Mac went home that day, he took another pile of Coco's colored eggs. "Same time tomorrow," he promised Bloo. "Three o'clock, right after school."

Little did Mac know that, across the street, his evil brother, Terrence, was hiding in the bushes. "He didn't get rid of that little blue jerk after all!" Terrence hissed. "He's sooo busted."

"So, you hate him, too," came a voice from behind him.

Terrence looked up and saw . . . "Ugh!" he said as Duchess stepped out from behind a tree.

"Leesen, you punk!" she said, shaking Terrence until his eyes spun. "You and I should hook up and get reed of zat leetle blue nuisance forever!"

"Hey," said Terrence. "Mac is my brother, and Bloo is his best friend. As much as I dislike him, I have *never* thought of doing something *so horrible* — it's a brilliant plan!" Terrence dropped to one knee and took Duchess's hand. "I am at your service, Your Horrible Hideousness."

The next day at three o'clock sharp, Bloo waited by the door for Mac.

"Don't worry," said Frankie. "He'll be here."

But Mac didn't come. He'd been on his way to Foster's when Terrence jumped out of the bushes. "I thought I'd walk my sweet little brother home," said Terrence. "So let's go!"

Mac tried to resist, but Terrence dragged Mac home, shoving him into his room. "I have to go!" yelled Mac.

"To the freaky weirdo house with all those freaky weirdos?" asked Terrence. "I know all about the Imaginary Friends up for adoption. In fact, there's one there I've got my eye on. He's cute, friendly, funny. . . ."

"Bloo!" Mac gasped.

Terrence shoved Mac into the closet and locked the door. He tossed the key on the dresser.

"Your plan won't work!" Mac yelled through the slats in the door. "They only adopt to nice kids, not jerks."

"Golly, shucks, Mac," Terrence said sweetly, putting on a nice-boy act. "I just want an Imaginary Friend of my very own. Mwa-ha-ha-ha!"

Mac pounded on the closet door, but it was no use. The door was locked, the key was on the dresser, and his mom wouldn't be home for hours. With Mac not there, Bloo could be adopted to anybody. Even Terrence. Defeated, Mac slid down to the floor in despair.

Meanwhile at Foster's, Bloo was heartbroken. It seemed Mac had forgotten him after all. Then there was a knock at the door. Bloo jumped up. "Mac!"

He ran to the door and opened it to find — oh, no! Terrence! Terrence with his hair combed and wearing a bow tie, trying to look like a good kid.

Duchess watched from the window. When she saw Terrence arrive, she went right out to the backyard to the cage of the Extremasaurus. With a snap of her red polished fingernails, she ordered the creature to snake one long tentacle out between the bars and pick her up. It did, and Duchess put her part of the plan into motion: she shrieked for help.

Hearing her screams, the friends went running outside to save Duchess from the

Extremasaurus. And just when Bloo needed them most.

"Help!" Duchess cried, pretending to be scared as her friend the Extremasaurus swung her around. "Vun of you eediots must save me!"

But the *real* monster was inside Foster's. Terrence had grabbed Bloo.

"May I help you?" asked Mr. Herriman, hopping into the foyer.

Terrence squeezed Bloo tight, showing that he really wanted to adopt this Imaginary Friend. Mr. Herriman checked his pocket watch. It was four o'clock. If Mac wasn't here by now, he thought, Bloo was free to be adopted. He beckoned Terrence to his office.

Back at home, Mac had not given up. He had a whole pile of Coco's eggs in the closet with him. He opened them one by one. Inside, he found a magnet, some rope, and a skateboard. Thinking fast, Mac pushed the skateboard under

the closet with the magnet on top. He knocked it into the dresser in the hope that the key would fall off and be attracted to the magnet. It worked! But then the rope came loose so that Mac couldn't pull the skateboard back. Ugh!

In Mr. Herriman's office, Terrence was just signing the adoption form.

Outside, Frankie distracted the Extremasaurus with some raw meat. Duchess dropped into Eduardo's arms.

In the closet, Mac desperately opened one last egg and found . . .

"A key!"

Mac opened the closet door and ran as fast as he could toward Foster's.

Duchess had a key of her own. Now that everyone had gone back inside the house, she slipped back to the Extremasaurus and opened his cage. "Who's a vicious monster?" she cooed, backing slowly away. "Who's a good Extrema-

saurus? Who did a good job? Who's a good boy? Dat's right."

The Extremasaurus stomped out of the cage. It was eight stories high, with glowing red eyes and huge tentacles made of cannonballs.

"Mommy's got vun more job for you," coaxed the Duchess. "Yes, she does. Yes, she does."

When Mac arrived at Foster's, he banged open the door and rushed inside. Wilt, Coco, Eduardo, and Frankie were sitting on the stairs.

"Bloo's gone, Mac," said Frankie sadly. "He's . . . he's . . ."

"Been adopted!" wailed Eduardo, starting to cry.

"I know!" said Mac. "That's just it! The kid who adopted Bloo was my horrible older brother, Terrence!"

Everyone gasped.

"But what I can't figure out is, how did he do it? Terrence is way too stupid to come up with this plan on his own. Somebody else must want to get rid of Bloo. But who?"

"Duchessss!" Frankie said. She led them out to the Extremasaurus's cage. It was empty.

Meanwhile, in a dark, creepy junkyard, Bloo was struggling to get out of Terrence's grip. "So, Bloofus," said Terrence. "Prepare to meet your DOOOOOOM!"

Duchess tottered out of the shadows on her high heels. "Surprise," she said to Bloo, holding tight to the Extremasaurus's chain. "I'll bet

you never vould have guessed it vas ME behind dees leetle scheme all da time!"

"Um, no, I wouldn't," said Bloo. "Who are you, again? I know you live at the house. . . . Was it Queenie? Princess?"

"It's Duchess! DUCHESS!!" she announced, full of fury. "And you have foiled my plans for da last time!"

She lashed the chain on the ground.

The Extremasaurus rose up until it towered behind Duchess.

"Awesome!" yelled Terrence. "That is so cool."

Duchess smiled. "Eet gets cooler," she said. She snapped her fingers. The Extremasaurus opened its huge, bright red mouth and roared. It smashed a heavy tentacle into the ground. Duchess snapped her fingers once more. "Sic 'em."

The Extremasaurus tore after Bloo.

"*Aaahhhh!*" Bloo ran as fast as his little blue body could go around piles of metal junk, car

parts, and spare tires. The Extremasaurus was right behind him, roaring and making the ground shake with every step it took.

The Extremasaurus came closer, snapping its huge metal jaws. "Good-bye, Mac!" Bloo cried. "Good-bye forever!"

LET'S BLOO THIS!

B loo!" a familiar voice called out.

Bloo looked around. He knew he heard Mac, but where was he? Bloo looked up and finally saw him. Mac was riding to the rescue with the other Imaginary Friends on a herd of flying unicorns. "I told you I'd be back."

Terrence laughed and pointed up at Mac. "Nice unicorns, ladies!" he yelled.

Mac leaped off the unicorns's back. He was ready for action. "All right, guys," he said, punching his fist into the air. "Let's *bloo* this!"

Nobody could believe Mac would say such a silly line at such a crucial moment. Even Terrence thought it was dumb. But there was no

time for apologies. The Extremasaurus was preparing to attack.

"Raaauuugh!" the Extremasaurus roared. The Imaginary Friends scattered in fear of the horrible beast.

"Dat's a good boy," said Duchess, encouraging her creature. "Get dem all. Da less competition, da better."

Bloo was in trouble, and Mac needed help to save him — but everyone was hiding from the Extremasaurus.

The Extremasaurus's cannonball tentacles slammed down beside Mac. That gave him an idea. He ran right underneath the Extremasaurus.

"Mac, are you crazy?" Bloo shrieked.

"No," said Mac. A tentacle grabbed him and raised him into the air. It whipped him back and forth. "Trust! Me!" Mac yelled as he was jerked from side to side. "I! Have! An! Idea! Watch! This! Heeeeeeelp!" Mac swung back and forth in the air, acting like he was caught by

the Extremasaurus. "Save me!"

"*Rooooowwwwwwrrr!*" Eduardo roared, charging the monster. He grabbed one of its heavy tentacles and pulled on the cannonball at the end. The cannonballs split apart like a string of beads. Mac fell down into Eduardo's waiting arms.

The cannonballs suddenly sprouted lit fuses and exploded. Eduardo and Mac shot into the air.

"I had no idea it deed dat!" said Duchess, impressed with the Extremasaurus.

Mac landed on a pile of colored eggs. In a panic, Coco was laying them all over the junkyard.

Another bunch of cannon-ball bombs were bouncing closer and closer to Eduardo, surrounding him.

But Mac had another idea and began shouting

out orders. "Eduardo — the tentacles! Wilt — the bombs! Coco — lay more eggs!"

Mac opened an egg, letting the alarm clock inside fall to the ground. Eduardo yanked on the Extremasaurus's tentacle. Cannonballs scattered everywhere. Wilt scooped one up and, with a stylish basketball move, passed it smoothly to Mac. Mac caught it and shut it in the empty egg, where it exploded harmlessly.

Heave! Pass! *Boom!* Heave! Pass! *Boom!* Until the last bomb was destroyed.

At that moment, a multicolored bus screeched to a halt in the junkyard. The door flung open. "That was amazing!" said Frankie, stepping out with Mr. Herriman.

"Quite," said the rabbit. Even *he* was impressed with what he saw.

But the battle wasn't over.

"*Aaaaaauuuuggh!*" Bloo was still being chased by what was left of the Extremasaurus, which was now a big round head with a mouth full of giant, sharp, pointed metal teeth.

Duchess and Terrence laughed from across the junkyard, pleased that their evil plot to destroy Bloo was working.

But Mac knew just what to do. He shot a giant spitball and hit Terrence right in the face. With Terrence in pursuit, Mac ran up alongside Bloo, just a few steps in front of the Extremasaurus.

"Wait!" Terrence yelled, running after Mac. "Stop! I just wanna punch you!"

"I think we need to split up," Mac announced to Bloo.

Bloo was stunned. "What? Now's the time you pick to abandon me?"

"No, I mean *split up*," Mac said. "You go left and I go right!" When they reached a corner, the two friends went in different directions.

And Terrence stopped short — right in front of the Extremasaurus. It opened its mouth and roared.

"*Aaaaauuuughh!*" yelled Terrence. He ran toward Duchess. "Tell it to stop! Tell it to stop!"

"Very vell," she said. "St —"

But before she could finish, two vases just like Mom's came crashing down from above her. Duchess and Terrence were knocked out cold. Wilt and Frankie grinned down at them, holding empty Coco eggs.

The Extremasaurus gobbled up Terrence and Dutchess.

Mac was only too happy to be rid of his brother, but he didn't know how he'd explain that to his mother. Luckily the Extremasaurus didn't like the

bad taste Terrence and Duchess left in its mouth and threw them right back up again.

Safely back at Foster's, Mr. Herriman apologized to Mac for doubting his devotion to Bloo. Then he gave Duchess the worst punishment she could imagine — making her stay at Foster's.

"But what about Bloo?" asked Mac.

"Well," said Mr. Herriman, "I am sorry to say that rules are rules!"

"Rules, schmools. Are you crazy?" screeched Frankie. "Let him stay!"

Frankie was continuing to yell at Herriman when suddenly there was a light *tap tap tap* on the stairs. The room went silent as a tiny old

lady came down the steps. She had a bun on her head almost taller than she was and big round glasses that made her eyes look huge.

"Madame Foster!" Bloo yelled in amazement. "You're alive!"

"Well, of course I am! It just takes me a while to get down the steps, okay? I am old!"

Madame Foster toddled quickly over to Mac and Bloo. "Okey-dokey," she said, coming up to Mac. "Hear you got a problem."

Madame Foster looked deep into Mac's eyes. And there she saw something that impressed her. "Ooh!" she said. "You've got it! I haven't seen an imagination as pure as that since . . . since me! Ha-ha-ha! Now, let's see about your little friend."

Madame Foster looked deep into Bloo's eyes. Again, she was amazed. "You are a true

friend!" she chuckled. "And SO CUTE I WANNA SQUEEZE YA!" She squeezed Bloo around the middle like a tube of toothpaste, then dropped him to the floor. "Okay," she said. "Bloo can live here and he won't ever be adopted. As long as Mac promises to visit him every day."

"You rock, Grandma!" shouted Frankie. She threw her arms around Madame Foster.

"But, Madame!" sputtered Mr. Herriman. "The house rules clearly state —"

"Oh, pooh, you and your rules!" said Madame Foster, turning to Mac and Bloo. "Ever since I imagined him when I was a little girl, he's been nothing but a hot crossed bunny!" She toddled over quickly and gave Mr. Herriman a hug. "But I love my Funny Bunny!"

Mac and Bloo couldn't believe it. Funny old Madame Foster had created stodgy Mr. Herriman when she was a little girl — and he was *still* her best friend!

"See, Mac, what did I tell ya?" said Bloo.

"Bringing me here was the perfect plan. It was just a little more of a hassle than we thought. So you'll be back tomorrow, right?"

"Maybe," said Mac with a shrug. "I might have things to do."

Bloo stared at his best friend in shock until he realized Mac was joking. Bloo gave Mac a playful shove.

Mac laughed. Bloo laughed. Wilt laughed. Eduardo and Coco laughed. In fact, everyone laughed at this wonderful, fun-derful imagination habitation.

Except Mr. Herriman, that is. He would have none of it. "Everyone, please be quiet now!" he shouted. "That is enough of this silly nonsense!"